LOST IN THE END

LOST MINECRAFT JOURNALS
BOOK THREE

Winter Morgan

Sky Pony Press
New York

Sky Pony Press books may be purchased in bulk at special discounts for
sales promotion, corporate gifts, fund-raising, or educational purposes.
Special editions can also be created to specifications. For details, contact
the Special Sales Department, Sky Pony Press, 307 West 36th Street,
11th Floor, New York, NY 10018 or info@skyhorsepublishing.com.

Sky Pony® is a registered trademark of Skyhorse Publishing, Inc.®,
a Delaware corporation.

Minecraft® is a registered trademark of Notch Development AB.
The Minecraft game is copyright © Mojang AB.

Visit our website at www.skyponypress.com.

10 9 8 7 6 5 4 3 2 1

Library of Congress Cataloging-in-Publication Data is available on file.

Cover photo by Megan Miller

Print ISBN: 978-1-5107-0352-0
Ebook ISBN: 978-1-5107-0355-1

Printed in Canada

TABLE OF CONTENTS

LOST IN THE END

1

WELCOME TO THE JUNGLE

Oliver hid behind a tree. His heart was pounding. He took a deep breath and peeked from behind the oak's dark-colored bark. He didn't see any of his friends. He wanted to call out to see if Julian and Ezra were close by, but he didn't want to draw attention to himself. He wondered if the others were destroyed. Maybe Charles or Valentino had trapped them? He wasn't sure. Oliver was glad he had survived the attack, but he missed his friends. The sky was getting dark, and he knew he had to find a place to stay. He couldn't stay hidden behind the tree forever. He was about to walk out from behind the tree, when an arrow pierced his arm. He began to cry out in pain. He was terrified.

"Ouch!" Oliver grabbed his sword, ready to fight his attacker. Oliver leapt from behind the oak tree, but began to shake when he saw a horde of bony skeletons standing in front of him. They aimed their arrows at him. There was no way he could fight back, but he tried. He swung his diamond sword at a skeleton. Before he could strike the undead mob, he was destroyed.

"Oliver's here," Harriet called out to the others. She stood over him as he respawned.

Oliver was confused. "What happened?"

"You were the last one to respawn. Charles destroyed us all. Luckily he didn't set us to Hardcore mode like he said he would, or we'd be gone for good," explained Harriet.

Ezra paced around the small house. "We need to get to the jungle. We have to find William and Sean."

"We've been over this a million times. We have no idea what jungle William could be in," Toby argued.

Jack interrupted, "Or if he is even in the jungle. He could still be in the End."

Veronica added, "And he could have been destroyed in the End. There is a possibility that William is gone and we've been on a wild goose chase."

Oliver shuddered and shouted, "How can you even say such a thing? William is still alive and we're going to find him."

Harriet said, "If we only had more pages from his journal, I'd feel more hopeful. It's just that we've been searching for so long and visited so many jungles and we haven't found him yet."

"We can't give up," said Oliver.

"But I don't want to be destroyed by Charles," Harried retorted. "I feel like we battle him everyday and lose. It's exhausting and it's making me sad."

Veronica looked at Harriet. "We can't give up hope. We have come so far. Think of all the jungle biomes we visited and we haven't found a trace of William and Sean's house. That means we don't have that many more to search. We will find them soon. The hard part is almost over."

Oliver studied his maps of the Overworld. "Look at these. I've noted all of the jungle biomes that we've visited. There is another jungle biome not far from here."

The group gathered around Oliver and looked at the map. Julian said, "I think we should head there in the morning. All we have to do is walk up a mountain and we'll be in the jungle."

They climbed into their beds and dreamt about finding William. They were hopeful this would be the jungle where they'd find him or discover clues that would lead them to him.

In the morning, Julian hunted for a chicken, and Jack and Toby gathered fruit for everyone. They ate an enormous feast before the journey to the jungle. When they finished eating, they put on their armor and walked into the sunny day.

"It's just over this mountain." Oliver pointed to the enormous mountain in the distance.

"Wow, you act like it's so easy to get over that mountain. It's going to take a lot of energy," said Toby.

"But it's worth it." Oliver looked at the map.

The trek up the side of the mountain was slow, and they quickly grew tired. They took a break and ate some apples.

"It's not that much further," Oliver pointed out, showing them the map.

The mountain's peak offered incredible views of the Overworld, but the group was too tired to enjoy it. They wanted to get to the jungle as quickly as they could, but the trip down was also quite slow.

"We don't want to trip and fall," Harriet reminded them as they climbed down the mountain.

"The jungle!" Toby called to the others, spotting it in the distance.

When they reached the bottom of the mountain, they were in a lush, green jungle biome.

"I'll clear a path for us." Oliver took out his shears.

The group followed Oliver through the dense jungle. Toby called out, "I see a jungle temple."

The gang sprinted toward the temple, as Harriet shouted, "I hope it has treasure chests!"

As they entered the enormous temple, they quietly and carefully explored each room. They kept a lookout for treasure hunters who might want to battle them.

"It looks like nobody is here." Harriet was relieved. "Let's find the treasure."

They walked downstairs toward the three stone bricks and levers. Oliver stood by the piston-trapped door and unleashed the treasure. As he opened the first treasure chest, Harriet called out.

"Come over here, guys." Harriet was in the corner of the dark jungle temple's basement. "I found something!"

"But we have a treasure chest to open," Veronica shouted back. She wanted Oliver to open the chest. She was excited to see what great treasures were hidden inside.

"Forget the treasure," Harriet exclaimed. "This is more important."

They sprinted toward Harriet. She looked at them and with a big grin, she pointed to a book. She picked it up. "It's the third journal. It looks shorter than the others."

The gang was elated. "Read it!" said Julian.

Veronica asked, "Should we open the treasure chest first?"

Harriet paused. "I guess we should open the chest."

Oliver opened the chest. "Diamonds!"

The group gathered the diamonds and placed them in their inventories.

"Good," said Harriet. "Now that that's settled, let's read." And Harriet began to read from the journal.

2

JOURNAL ENTRY: DRAGON BATTLE

Entry 1: Dragon's Breath

The End room was the last place I wanted to be, but there was no way out of the stronghold. I looked over at Sean and asked, "We have to go back to the End, don't we?"

Sean nodded and I followed him onto the portal. A purple mist filled the room. We could hear the people in black shouting, but the voices went quiet. We were out of the stronghold and in the End. As we stood on the obsidian pillar, we saw the mammoth scaly dragon fly toward us. It swept down and struck Sean with its gray wing.

"Are you okay?" I asked.

Sean breathlessly replied that he was fine and quickly grabbed milk from his inventory and drank it.

I grabbed a snowball from my inventory and struck the Ender Dragon, depleting a portion of the dragon's health bar. I was beginning to feel confident that we might win the battle and respawn in the Overworld, but the dragon flew to a pillar and the Ender crystals shot a ray toward the dragon. Within seconds the dragon had a full health bar, and lunged toward us at great speed.

"Watch out!" I called to Sean.

Sean shot an arrow at the powerful dragon, piercing its side. The dragon was infuriated and continued flying toward us.

We sprinted from the dragon and tried to hide behind an obsidian pillar, but we couldn't escape. The dragon crashed into the pillar. We sprinted further away, but the dragon followed.

"What are we going to do?" I asked Sean.

Sean threw a snowball at the dragon and hit its face. "I don't have many snowballs left in my inventory. I'm afraid this is the End, my friend."

"Don't say that," I replied, and grabbed a snowball and aimed at the weakened dragon. "We just need to destroy the Ender crystals and then the dragon won't have a way of regenerating its health bar."

"Good plan!" Sean shot an arrow at the Ender crystals, as the Ender Dragon was regaining strength from them.

Kaboom! The fiery purple crystals exploded. The Ender Dragon was hurt by the explosion and lost ten hearts.

Sean was saving us from the Ender Dragon! We sprinted from the weak dragon, but didn't get very far. As we trekked deeper into the dark End, we saw a gang of Endermen approach us.

I warned Sean, "Don't stare at them."

"It's too late," Sean cried out, as two Endermen shrieked and teleported toward him.

"Sprint!" I shouted to Sean. I had no other plan and I just wanted to escape from the End.

We sprinted, but the Endermen followed us. I leapt at the Endermen, striking the lanky beasts with my diamond sword, but it takes a lot to destroy an Enderman, and we didn't have enough energy left to put up a good fight.

Just when I was ready to give up, Sean splashed a potion of invisibility on us and we fled the Endermen. As we sprinted away, Sean said, "The only way out of here is defeating the Ender Dragon. We can't waste our energy running away—we have to battle the dragon or be destroyed. There are no other options."

I knew Sean was right. Running away from the hostile mobs of the End was pointless. We needed to run toward them and defeat them or at least try to defeat them. We turned around and used our only powerful weapon, our invisibility, to defeat thee mobs. As I threw snowballs at the Ender Dragon, Sean destroyed the Ender crystals.

"Shoot them now!" I shouted at Sean. The dragon was flying close to the crystals.

Kaboom! The explosion weakened the dragon.

I was hopeful. "I think we're going to make it!"

"Don't be too sure," a familiar voice called out.

I almost dropped my bow and arrow. It was Charles, and he let out a sinister laugh that was so loud it almost drowned out the noise from the exploding Ender crystals.

"What are you doing here?" I asked

Charles laughed again. "I am here to destroy you. I've used command blocks to put you on Hardcore mode. Be prepared to meet your end in the End." He laughed even harder at his awful pun.

"Never!" I shouted. I aimed my arrow at Charles and struck him.

"Don't waste your time with him," Sean cried out. "Save the arrows for the Ender Dragon. I just have one more Ender crystal to destroy and then we can corner the dragon."

I listened to Sean. I shot arrows at the Ender Dragon as Sean destroyed the last Ender crystal. The final explosion destroyed the Ender Dragon. A Dragon egg and a portal to the Overworld spawned in front of us.

"We're saved!" I looked over at Sean, as we walked toward the portal to the Overworld. Charles followed us.

"You're not coming back to the Overworld with us," Sean told Charles.

Charles laughed again. "Yes, I am." He held a diamond sword against Sean's chest. Sean's energy level was dangerously low, and we were worried Charles could destroy him.

As we walked onto the portal and read the End Poem, we were happy to return to the Overworld. We weren't happy that we were traveling back with our enemy. When we emerged in the jungle, I grabbed a potion of strength and drank it and then handed the potion to Sean. With our energy restored, we attacked Charles.

I demanded, "Tell me where you are hiding Oliver."

Charles just laughed harder. He didn't even try to fight back.

Sean warned, "We have to stop fighting him. We don't want to destroy him; we want to capture him and find out where his minions are hiding."

It was too late. I had struck Charles with my diamond sword until he was destroyed.

"I'm sorry," I said to Sean.

"It's okay." Sean looked around the jungle. He was hoping it was the same biome where we had built our home, but it didn't look familiar at all.

We didn't have time to explore. The sky grew dark and a skeleton army approached us and began to attack. A sea of arrows hit us. In order to survive, we sprinted as fast as we could, until we reached the shore. Sean handed me a potion of underwater breathing. We both drank the potion and jumped into the deep blue water.

3
SURPRISES

K eep reading," demanded Veronica.

"There isn't anything else. That was it!" Harriet told them. "I told you it was short."

"Seriously? That's it?" Veronica was annoyed. This didn't give them any answers. She wanted an exact location for William.

"We have to head to the shore and search for William," Harriet told the group.

"Which means we don't have to travel to the End." Oliver was relieved. It was too scary and he disliked battling the Ender Dragon.

The only person who seemed annoyed was Jack. "Another wild goose chase. The Overworld is covered in water. How are we going to find the spot where William jumped into the water? This is just going to end like all the other searches have ended."

"But we can't give up hope," Harriet reminded him. "We have come too far. There's no point in turning back now."

Jack sighed. "I'm just tired of searching for William. When we found the first journal, I was excited, but now I am growing bored. You can't blame me, it's been a long time and we haven't even gotten close to finding him."

Oliver looked at Jack. "If you gave up right away, you wouldn't have found me."

Harriet stood next to Oliver. "We found Oliver. And soon we will find William. They will be reunited and the Overworld will celebrate their return and hear all about their new explorations."

Veronica exclaimed, "And we'll be famous!"

"Veronica"—Harriet was annoyed—"I told you. We aren't doing this for the credit. We are trying to find William because it's the right thing to do and will benefit everyone in the Overworld."

"Oh yeah," Veronica said, "I forgot."

Ezra announced, "There's no point in arguing about this any longer. It's just a waste of time. Let's start by searching beneath the sea."

Oliver took out his map and showed it to the group. "I see a large body of water, just beyond this jungle. We should explore that area."

"Let's head there now," ordered Harriet.

"But it's almost dusk," said Julian. "We need to build a place to stay in the jungle."

Ezra looked around. "Can't we just stay here? We can craft beds in this jungle temple."

"No, it isn't safe here. Hostile mobs can spawn in the temple," Jack warned them.

The gang left the temple and looked for somewhere to build a house. Spotting a small patch of land in the distance, Harriet said, "That looks like a good place to build."

The gang sprinted toward the patch of land and began to craft the house. Harriet grabbed wooden planks and constructed a wall.

"This is happening a lot faster than I imagined," Jack said as he constructed the door.

"I know!" Harriet was excited. "We'll be done soon, and we can rest up before our journey to the sea."

The group worked quickly and the house was almost completed when Veronica shouted, "Ouch!"

Valentino and his army, dressed in black, stood in front of the group, attacking them with arrows, swords, and splash potions.

"You can't sleep here now," Valentino laughed as he ordered his soldiers to blow up the house with TNT.

"No! Stop!" Harriet pleaded.

"Blow it up!" Valentino cried to his army.

Kaboom! The house was gone.

"You aren't going to get away with this!" Julian struck Valentino with his diamond sword.

Valentino lunged at Julian, as he ordered his soldiers to attack the group. "Destroy them all!"

The soldiers used all of their weapons to fight the gang, but the group fought back. Jack plunged his sword into a soldier and destroyed him. Toby threw a potion of harming on the soldiers and weakened them. As they stood motionless, Harriet and Veronica destroyed them.

"My army!" Valentino cried.

"You'll never win, Valentino!" Veronica shouted at her old friend.

"Traitor!" Valentino shouted.

Veronica rushed toward Valentino and delivered a final blow with her diamond sword. Valentino was destroyed.

The sky was growing darker. The group stood by the remains of their jungle home. Harriet walked around the charred remains of the house. "What are we going to do?"

Julian looked up at the sky, it was almost dark and hostile mobs would be spawning soon. "We're going to rebuild. And we're going to do it as fast as we can."

The group worked quickly to finish the house before dark. Ezra kept an eye for hostile mobs that might be spawning in the jungle as the others worked on the house.

"What's this?" Harriet asked.

"What's what?" asked Jack.

Harriet picked up a book that was on the ground. "It's *another* journal! William must have broken up this last journal into a bunch of journals!"

The gang gathered around her. Julian reminded them, "We can read this once we finish the house. But we can't leave ourselves exposed. We could be attacked at any minute."

The group put the roof on the house, and then placed a torch on the front of the home to ward off hostile mobs. They crafted beds and once they were tucked in, Harriet began to read.

4
JOURNAL ENTRY: UNDER THE SEA

Entry 2: The Water

We swam through the deep blue ocean until we found a large ocean monument. I swam as fast as I could toward the large underwater temple, but I spotted a guardian swimming past me. I tried to avoid contact with the one-eyed fish, but it already had me on its radar. The spiky fish focused its single eye on me and shot a laser in my direction. I was struck.

"Help!" I cried to Sean. I was fatigued from the strike. Sean swam to my side and gave me some milk.

I drank the milk while Sean shot an arrow at the guardian and it was destroyed.

"I see a bunch of guardians heading our way," Sean warned me. He handed me a potion for night vision and swiftness. "These will help us see and swim faster; it's our only hope for survival. If we are destroyed under the water, we'll lose everything and it will make living in the Overworld extremely difficult."

I drank the potions and followed Sean to the bottom of the ocean. "Where are we going?" I asked him.

"We need to get away from the guardians. If they can't see us, they can't attack us."

"But why are we swimming to the bottom of the ocean? Shouldn't we just swim to the surface and head back to the Overworld?" I was confused. I wasn't sure what Sean had in mind for us. I just wanted to get back to the Overworld and defeat Charles and find Oliver and the friends we had lost. I wondered what happened to Molly, Esther, and Thao.

Sean continued swimming and explained. "If we dig a tunnel on the ocean's floor, we can access the ocean monument from there."

Sean took out a pickaxe and dug a tunnel on the bottom of the ocean floor. I joined him, and we dug a deep tunnel and made our way into the ocean monument. We entered through a room filled with gold blocks in dark prismarine.

"Gold!" I called out. I was excited. We could fill our inventories with gold and use it to trade in the Overworld.

Sean grabbed some gold bars and placed them in his inventory and I did the same. But when I looked up, I saw an elder guardian enter the room. "Oh no!" Sean called out. He shot an arrow at the elder guardian, but the arrow missed the fish.

"I've got it." I shot at the fish, but it swam swiftly away from the floating arrow.

The Elder Guardian focused its menacing eye on us and began to shoot its laser. We were both struck with Mining Fatigue.

"We need milk," Sean said weakly.

We took milk from our inventories and began to drink. We were tired and knew this battle wasn't going to be easy. Defeating the elder guardian wasn't an easy job. I wished our friends were there to help. I wished we were rescuing Oliver from the desert. I wished we were anywhere besides trying to battle this pesky fish that was guarding this temple.

I hid behind gold bricks and shot another arrow at the elder guardian. It struck him. Sean shot another arrow, which pierced the side of the fish.

Sean said, "It's weakened. We have to keep shooting arrows."

I listened and shot as many arrows as I could. I was glad when the elder guardian was destroyed.

"Now we're safe to explore the ocean monument," Sean told me, and we made our way through the massive underwater temple.

"Aren't there three elder guardians in each ocean monument?" I asked.

"Yes, but we've defeated one. If we keep an eye out for the others, we'll be fine."

I carefully looked around for guardians. I didn't believe we were truly safe. We had lived under the water before, and although Sean was more familiar with the landscape and a lot more confident beneath the sea, I knew there were many dangers there.

We swam through the prismarine monument lit by sea lanterns, and while I kept an eye out for fish, I asked Sean, "How long should we stay here? We have our gold and are away from Charles. We don't need to live here though, right?"

Sean took out his potion for underwater breathing and handed me some. "We don't want to run low on this."

I drank the potion. "You didn't answer my question. How long do you want to stay here? I want to swim to the surface and leave."

"I think we should finish looting this ocean monument, and then we can head back to the Overworld. How does that sound?"

I told him that was okay, and swam as fast as I could through the ocean monument. I wanted to get out of there.

I was distracted, caught up in my thoughts, when Sean shouted, "Watch out!"

The second elder guardian had spotted us and staged an attack. Sean was already struck by the laser and had Mining Fatigue. I swam to his side and gave him some milk.

"Thanks," Sean said as he grabbed his bow and arrow and struck the elder guardian.

We both shot arrows at the second elder guardian. When the fish was finally destroyed, I shouted at Sean, "I want to leave. I don't want to battle another fish. We already have gold. I don't want to loot this place; I want to swim back to the Overworld."

I was shocked when a familiar voice said, "Are you two fighting?"

It was Charles, and he let out a sinister laugh.

We didn't have to battle another fish. We had to battle our worst enemy.

5

THE ATTACK OF THE
ELDER GUARDIANS

We will travel to the ocean tomorrow morning," Harriet said as she put the journal down and got ready for bed.

"Don't you think it's odd that we found the journal after we fought Valentino? I was thinking this journal might be a hoax," Julian told the group. "It could be leading us on a wild goose chase and further from where William is living, if William is still alive."

"Don't say that!" Oliver was upset. "Don't say that William isn't alive. That's awful. I know we will find him, just like you guys found me. I know I'll be reunited with my old friend."

"Tomorrow we'll travel beneath the sea. Even if we don't find William, it will be an adventure. And maybe we can find some gold blocks," Veronica told the group.

They all fell asleep dreaming of finding William. Harriet dreamt that they discovered William in the ocean monument and they threw a huge party in the Overworld. She imagined the cake at the party. They were all excited to find William. When they woke up, they ate breakfast and prepared for their trip to the shore.

"Do we have enough potions for underwater breathing?" Jack asked the group.

Everyone checked their inventories and determined that they had enough supplies. "I also have a lot of potions for swiftness and night vision, which could come in handy," said Harriet.

"That's good to know," said Jack as they walked closer to the shore.

Harriet looked at the blue water. It seemed as if the sea was endless. She stopped on the shore. "Wow. He could be anywhere in this ocean."

"We have to start somewhere," Ezra said. He was the first to take a drink of the potion of underwater breathing. He jumped into the deep blue water.

The others followed. Ezra swam and they followed him further into the ocean.

"There's a guardian," shouted Veronica.

The group sipped the potion of swiftness and quickly got out of the guardian's path.

"That was close," Veronica said to the group.

The gang swam for a while, but they didn't spot an ocean monument. They were losing hope that they would find one and even more so that they would ever discover William in this vast ocean.

"Oliver, do you have a map for the ocean?" asked Harriet.

"No. I wish I did. William and I never explored the ocean as much as we wanted to, so I don't have any detailed maps."

Jack told everyone they should drink the potion for night vision. "I think that will help us spot ocean monuments."

They drank the potion and swam deeper into the blue ocean, but they still couldn't find an ocean monument.

"Maybe we should just swim back to the Overworld?" suggested Toby.

"No, we've come too far. We have to give it a little more time," said Jack as he swam through the ocean biome.

"I think I see something." Veronica's voice was shaky.

"An ocean monument?" asked Harriet.

"No! Look!" Veronica shouted as a swarm of guardians raced toward them.

"That's unusual; they don't usually travel in large schools," said Oliver, watching the mobs approach.

"I bet Valentino or Charles summoned them," said Jack as he grabbed his bow and arrow and began to shoot at the fish.

"Do you think we can hide?" asked Harriet.

"We don't have time to hide," shouted Toby, "we have to fight."

The group used their strength to battle the one-eyed fish with deadly laser beams.

"I have Mining Fatigue," Harriet called out. "Help! I don't have any milk."

Jack swam toward Harriet and gave her some milk, but was struck by a guardian's laser and also grew extremely tired. He sipped some of the milk himself to regain his energy.

The gang dodged blasts from the guardians as they shot arrows at the fish. They had destroyed several of the guardians, but there were still many left to battle. They were all losing energy and had depleted health bars.

"We can't keep this up too much longer," Jack said as he destroyed another guardian.

"And we haven't even found an ocean monument," Harriet cried out as she was struck from another guardian laser.

They were about to give up. Toby suggested they each drink a potion of swiftness and swim as fast as they could toward the surface. They had all agreed that was a great idea, when Harriet called out, "Wait! I see something!"

Through the swarm of one-eyed guardians, Harriet saw a prismarine ocean monument. The group had a second burst of energy. They were ready to defeat the remaining fish and to swim toward the monument. With their last bit of energy, the gang shot arrows at the guardians and destroyed them.

"We did it!" Harriet called out. She was relieved the battle was over and she was excited to explore the ocean monument. She hoped that William was in the monument, but knew that was a long shot.

The gang swam toward the entrance, but an elder guardian emerged from the underwater temple and attacked them.

"We can defeat one elder guardian," Harriet said quite confidently, "after we just defeated a neverending supply of guardians."

The battle of the sole elder guardian wasn't as easy as Harriet had imagined. The powerful fish had great strength and the group had to use many arrows to defeat it. When it was finally gone, they made their way into the temple.

"We should look for gold," said Veronica.

"We have to look for William," interrupted Oliver.

"We have to look for more elder guardians if we plan on surviving," Harriet reminded them both.

The group swam into the room where the gold bars were kept in dark prismarine, but the room had been emptied.

"It looks like this place has already been looted." They were all disappointed.

Oliver looked down on the ground and picked up a book. "This can't be."

The gang gathered around Oliver.

Harriet asked, "What did you find?"

"It's another journal." Oliver looked through the book.

"Read it, Oliver," Veronica instructed.

They all took sips from their potions of underwater breathing and Oliver began to read the book.

6

JOURNAL ENTRY:
OLD ENEMIES AND FRIENDS

Entry 3: Reunions

I knew we were running low on underwater breathing potions and I didn't want to battle Charles beneath the sea. But Sean took out his sword and struck Charles, and we had to finish the battle. I worried Charles wasn't alone and we'd be forced to fight his army.

"How did you find us?" I shouted at Charles as Sean attacked him with his diamond sword.

"You weren't hard to find." Charles let out a boisterous laugh and lunged at Sean with his diamond sword.

"Where's your army?" I asked as I shot an arrow at him.

"They're here. I'm not going to battle you alone. So, there's no point in destroying me, when they are just going to annihilate you when I'm gone." He laughed even louder.

I could see an elder guardian swimming toward us. I shouted, "Sean, watch out!"

Sean swam toward me and we watched the elder guardian attack Charles. We used this as an opportunity to escape from the ocean biome. We both drank more potion of swiftness and swam to the surface. It took a while and I was exhausted. I was nervous that more guardians would attack us, and my heart was racing. When we finally reached the surface of the water, I was relieved.

"Air," I called out to Sean. "Fresh air."

Sean looked around. "But I don't see land. We're in the middle of the ocean. We need to find a shore."

We floated and swam for a while, but there was still no land. Then Sean called out, "I see two boats in the water."

As we grew closer, we could see that the boats were empty. I was excited and surprised by our find. We swam to the boats and hopped aboard.

"This is fantastic," I said as I relaxed on the boat and ate some apples I had in my inventory.

Sean agreed. He ate a potato and looked at the sun. "It's still daylight and this is very peaceful. But we need to make our way to the shore before nightfall."

I looked ahead. I could see a small island in the distance. "I think I see a Mushroom Island."

"You're right, that is a Mushroom Island!" Sean was happy to see land.

We steered the boats toward Mushroom Island and docked on the peaceful, picturesque shore. I spotted a mooshroom grazing peacefully on the grassy biome. Sean sprinted toward it.

"If we milk it, we can get mooshroom stew," he shouted back.

As he milked the mooshroom, I looked at the large red mushrooms that grew around the island. It was very scenic land. I had explored this island before with Oliver and we had both enjoyed our visit very much. We loved that hostile mobs didn't spawn there. It was a place where we could relax and regroup without fear of being attacked.

I looked over at Sean. "Maybe we should stay here awhile and try to come up with a plan to defeat Charles and find Oliver."

Sean handed me some mooshroom stew, and I thanked him. It was very tasty and I was beginning to feel hopeful.

"Yes," he agreed, "that sounds like a good idea. We can construct a house out of a mushroom! I've always wanted to live in a mushroom house."

Having both agreed that we should stay on Mushroom Island, we sipped our soup and relaxed. But I heard voices in the distance.

"There's someone else here. We're not alone," I warned Sean. "We have to go see who else is on the island."

"We don't know if these people want to attack us, so we have to be nice," Sean said.

Sean reminded me of Oliver. He was also a little too trusting. I assumed everyone was our enemy. I clutched my diamond sword as we searched for the sources of the voices. I wanted to be ready in case they attacked us. Sean didn't have a weapon in his hand; he trusted that they wouldn't attack.

"Esther!" Sean called out and sprinted toward the voices.

"Esther? Really?" I asked. I was shocked. I couldn't believe we were going to be reunited with our old friends.

Esther sprinted toward Sean. "Sean! I'm here with Molly and Thao."

Sean asked, "How did you guys wind up here?"

"We respawned here and decided to stay because it was peaceful. We thought it would be impossible to find you guys, so we built homes here and have been here ever since we lost you in the End."

Then Molly saw me. "Oh, it's William! I thought you guys were destroyed in the End. I was convinced that Charles put you both on Hardcore mode. I am so happy to see you. We must have a feast tonight."

Thao asked, "How did you guys get here?"

We told them about our adventures and the multiple trips to the End, our jungle house, and battling Charles under the sea. I felt like my old self, when Oliver and I would show up in various towns in the Overworld and tell people about our explorations. The group was excited to hear about how Sean and I had survived after we had parted from them.

"I'm so glad you're both safe." Esther smiled. "You can stay with us."

"Actually, we really wanted to build a house out of a mushroom," said Sean.

"You can do that," said Molly, "but we built a large castle."

Molly, Esther, and Thao walked us over to a mammoth castle that overlooked the water. I couldn't believe I hadn't spotted it when we arrived on the island. It was very opulent and colorful and had a large picture window and a deck.

"We'd love to stay here," I said.

Sean looked disappointed. He wasn't impressed with the large home; he wanted to build a house out of a mushroom. I was happy that this was our biggest problem. After being kept prisoner and battling Charles, I realized that deciding where we'd stay wasn't a big deal. So I said, "Sean, let's build the mushroom house."

"We'll help you," added Molly.

We gathered supplies and started to construct a mushroom house near their mansion.

As we put the finishing touches on the house, Thao shouted out. "Ouch."

We turned around and saw Charles and his army.

7
BACK TO THE OVERWORLD

I f the journal entry ends on Mushroom Island, how did it wind up under the sea?" asked Harriet.

"That's a good question. I think you we're right to suspect that this journal might be a hoax," Toby said.

Oliver wouldn't hear any of it. "We haven't finished reading the journal—maybe they don't stay on Mushroom Island! And anyway, there are lots of ways the journal could have ended up under the sea. We have to believe in the journal and we need to go back to the Overworld and to Mushroom Island. If we find William there, we're done searching."

Oliver swam toward the surface and the others followed him. When they reached the surface of the ocean, they saw a shore in the distance.

"It's not too far from the land," said Harriet. "We can make it."

The group swam as fast as they could and crawled onto the shore. Veronica saw a small village. "I see shops.

We should go into the village and trade some of our treasures for resources."

Everyone agreed. They were running low on resources and needed to replenish their supplies.

The village had a butcher, a blacksmith, and a library, but it was missing a golem. One of the villagers approached the group.

"Are you the people who have arrived to help us rebuild the golem?" they asked the gang.

"No, what happened to your golem?" asked Harriet.

"Somebody stole it, and ever since we've been having nightly zombie attacks. Sometimes they even come during the day when it's raining," the villager replied.

"That's awful," Harriet said. "Guys, I think we should help them."

"Thank you, we need all the help we can get. The zombies are awful and they have changed some of the villagers into zombies." The villager smiled.

Oliver asked his friends. "Do we have the supplies needed to build a golem?"

The gang looked through their inventories, but the villager interrupted. "Don't worry, we will provide the supplies. We just need your help building it."

The villager led them to the spot where the old golem had once stood. Other villagers joined them and thanked the group for helping build a golem.

Harriet grabbed the iron blocks and began to craft the golem, when she felt a drop on her head.

"Oh no," Harriet called out, "it's raining."

The sky grew dark and the rain began to fall on the village.

Then Oliver cried out, "Zombies!"

A gang of zombies lumbered toward the group, and began to rip doors off of the village shops.

"Help us!" cried the villagers.

Veronica lunged at two zombies with her diamond sword and struck them. Jack and Toby splashed the zombies with potions of harming. The others used arrows and swords to battle the zombies, but it was pointless. New zombies kept spawning and terrorizing the village.

Townspeople sprinted from their homes to help the gang and the defenseless villagers battle the zombies. The rain kept falling, and the gang used all of their resources to battle the undead mobs.

Oliver struck a zombie with his diamond sword, but he was losing energy fast. He tried to grab milk or a potion of strength from his inventory, but it was impossible. Every time he tried to access his inventory, a zombie attacked him. He cried out, "Someone help me. I only have a couple of hearts left."

Veronica sprinted toward his side. With one hand she skillfully battled a zombie and with the other hand she handed Oliver milk. He drank the milk and joined her back in battle.

When the rain finally stopped and the sun came out, the zombies disappeared. The villager said to the gang, "This is what happens all the time. We are under constant attack by zombies."

"We will help you," Harriet said again, more determined than ever.

The others looked at Harriet. They were happy she was so eager to help, but they worried this project would sidetrack them. They had a mission to accomplish. They needed to get to Mushroom Island to save William.

As they built the golem, Jack asked Oliver, "Do you have a map of this part of the Overworld? Do you happen to know how far Mushroom Island is from this town?"

One of the townspeople overheard Jack say "Mushroom Island" and interrupted them, "Did you say Mushroom Island? We just had some visitors who had come from that island, and they told us all about it."

"Who?" asked Harriet. She wondered if the visitors were William and his friends.

"They were two women. I think their names were Molly and Esther," the townsperson replied. "They were very nice. We liked having them here. That was before our golem was stolen and we were attacked by zombies."

"When did they leave?" asked Harriet.

"It wasn't that long ago." The townsperson paused. "I can't say I know the exact date, but I do know they were very nice."

As Harriet continued to work on the golem, she said to her friends, "I don't think they're still on Mushroom Island."

Everyone agreed. Oliver said, "We need to find the next journal. It's our only hope to finding William."

The townsperson said, "Journal? One of the women left a book at the library. I tried to read it, but it didn't make any sense at all. It was supposed to be an explorer's journal, but there was no plot and it started in the middle. I'm not a fan of that type of book."

"Where's the book?" asked Harriet.

"I left it at the library. I figured somebody else might enjoy it, and in case they ever came back and were looking for it, I thought we shouldn't throw it away."

Harriet asked, "Can you take me to the library? I want to see the book."

The townsperson led Harriet to the library. The librarian asked them if they needed help. The townsperson said, "I'm looking for that journal I had left here. I told you about it."

The librarian led them down an aisle of books and pulled out the journal. "Here it is."

Harriet thanked the librarian and left the library. She opened the book. Her friends crowded around as she read.

8

JOURNAL ENTRY: TRAPPED AGAIN

Entry 4: Prisoner on Mushroom Island

"This is our island!" Molly shouted at Charles.

Charles's boisterous laugh was loud, and he said, "This is the end for you guys."

I looked behind Charles and noticed more soldiers emerging from the grassy mushroom-lined landscape. I imagined they had either TPed to the island or Charles had constructed a series of boats. In any case, we were outnumbered. I tried to formulate an escape, but it was pointless.

Sean whispered to me, "Do we have any more potion of invisibility?"

I didn't have any in my inventory. I asked the others, but they didn't have any potions left either.

"We surrender." I held up my arms.

I noticed Molly and Esther were annoyed with me. They wanted to battle Charles, but I knew it would just weaken us and we'd be left in worse shape.

Charles led us toward the water. There was a large hole in the ground near the shore and he told us to climb inside. The hole led to a large stronghold. Charles's soldiers led us to a prison. They locked us in the cell. One of the soldiers laughed and bellowed, "Welcome to your new home."

The soldier left and we were alone in the small cell.

"Trapped again?" said Esther. "Charles won't get away with this."

We all agreed, but we didn't have a plan. We had to escape and we also had to defeat Charles.

"Now that we are trapped in here, we can use this time to come up with a plan."

Sean wasn't listening. He was too busy looking through his inventory. He said, "I have a pickaxe." He took out the pickaxe and dug a hole in the ground.

Thao warned him, "Stop. I hear the guard coming down the hall. If they see you digging a hole in the ground, they might destroy you."

"Yes, stop," chimed in Molly. "We never know what Charles is planning. He could have used command blocks to set us to Hardcore mode."

Thao used to work with Charles and he agreed. "Charles is always planning something awful. We need to watch out for him and we have to be smart about our next move."

I just wanted to escape from the prison cell. I couldn't believe that a few moments earlier, I had been happy. I had truly believed I could live a peaceful life on Mushroom Island, and now I was trapped in a prison. I was upset. I was annoyed. I was angry. When Charles walked toward our cell, I yelled, "Charles, we've had enough of this!"

Charles laughed. "I especially love capturing Thao. He was once an obedient soldier, but now he has his own ideas. What a silly man."

Thao was angry. "We are going to get out of here. You aren't going to win."

Charles let out another deep laugh. "You can talk about escaping and winning all you want. But remember, you are still my prisoner."

Charles left and Thao suggested, "I have a bunch of supplies. I think we should brew some potions. We have to use this time to be productive and plan our escape. If we have an inventory full of potions, we will have a better chance of getting out of here and surviving."

We all agreed with Thao, but we weren't sure how we could brew potions in our small cell when Charles and his soldiers were guarding us.

I hushed the group. "Shhh—listen. I can hear Charles talking."

The group stood quietly and listened. Charles was shouting at his soldiers. "We are running low on resources. We need to travel to the Nether to get supplies to brew potions. I don't trust our prisoners. They're smart and are probably planning an escape. We need to be prepared for battle."

I paced in the small cell. "This is good news. They aren't as strong as we thought. This is the best time to plan our escape."

"But how?" asked Esther.

We were interrupted by a horde of skeletons walking toward our jail cell. "I didn't think hostile mobs could spawn on Mushroom Island," I said.

Thao replied, "Charles must have summoned them. They want to weaken us. Or destroy us."

"Or distract us while they travel to the Nether," added Esther.

Luckily we still had weapons in our inventories. As I heard the sound of the skeletons' bones click, clack, clang, I grabbed my bow and arrow and aimed at the bony beasts.

"You've got it," Esther exclaimed as I struck a skeleton with an arrow.

The gang flooded the horde of skeletons with arrows, but they were strong and retaliated, aiming their arrows at us.

We dodged arrows as we fought the skeletons. It was a hard battle. There was no place to hide. We were trapped in the jail cell. I'm not sure how we defeated the skeletons. It seemed like a miracle when they were all gone. When the final skeleton was defeated, I ordered the group to eat and drink to replenish their energy. As we ate apples, potatoes, and carrots, we tried to come up with a plan.

Sean said, "I think the only way out of here is digging that hole."

The others agreed.

Sean began to dig the hole. When it was large enough, Molly and Esther were the first to crawl in the hole.

As they disappeared into the hole, Charles returned. "What are you doing?" he shouted.

"Nothing," I replied.

"Don't lie to me. I can see that Esther and Molly are missing," he shouted as he entered the jail cell. He walked toward the hole we had dug in the center of the jail cell and called out to Esther and Molly, but they did not reply.

I hoped they had emerged on Mushroom Island and were on a boat back to the mainland. I hoped they were far from here.

9
PEAKS AND VALLEYS

When did the women leave?" Harriet asked the townsperson.

"I told you, it wasn't that long ago. I don't remember the exact date. But it was before the zombie attacks started. So you understood the book? I didn't enjoy it at all."

Before Harriet could answer, Julian cut in. "How did the book get here? William must have written that entry when they left. I'm very confused."

The gang stood by Harriet and looked over her shoulder. They analyzed the journal.

Ezra said, "I don't think Esther and Molly escaped that time."

Everyone agreed. There was something missing. But they all knew it was a possibility that William could still be trapped on Mushroom Island.

"We should go to Mushroom Island," Harriet told her friends.

The townsperson said, "You can't leave without help-ing us finish the golem. You guys were doing such a fan-tastic job and we need the help. We are being destroyed by these nightly zombie attacks."

Harriet looked up at the sky. It was dusk. They would have to spend the night in the town anyway, because it would be too dangerous to travel at night. "If you give us a place to stay," she said, "we will help you fight the zombies and construct the golem."

The townsperson thanked them. "I have room on my wheat farm. It's not far from here."

The gang followed him to his wheat farm. Harriet said, "You never told us your name."

"I'm Steve," he replied, as he led them out of the town and toward his farm.

The farm was quite lush and his house was very large. There was more than enough room for every-one in his farmhouse. Steve's walls were adorned with emeralds.

"You have a very nice house," Julian remarked. "I also live in a town that is similar to this one, but my wheat farm isn't as nice as this one."

Steve was very modest. "This farm isn't that nice. I don't travel much. I'd rather spend my time on the farm. Since I have a lot of carrots and wheat, I'm able to trade with village shops and have lots of resources."

Harriet was excited to hear that Steve had lots of resources. They were running low and needed all the help they could get for their battle with both Charles and Valentino. Harriet said, "If we help you battle this zombie invasion, would you help us battle the man who is trapping our friend?"

"Of course," Steve said, but added, "I'm not really a fighter. I usually like to stay close to home."

"Well, you can help us. You have many resources and we need to battle a man who is trapping William the Explorer," explained Harriet.

"William the Explorer!" Steve was shocked. "I used to idolize him and read about all of his explorations with Oliver."

Oliver introduced himself. "I'm Oliver. I was William's fellow explorer."

"No way! I can't believe I'm meeting Oliver! This is the most exciting thing that has ever happened to me!" Steve was beaming.

There was a banging on the door and Harriet called out, "It's zombies. One of them is yanking the door off the hinge!"

Steve took out a diamond sword. Everyone prepared themselves for the zombie attack.

When the zombie ripped the door off of Steve's house, the group was speechless. There were countless zombies standing in front of them.

"How are we going to defeat them?" Steve's voice was shaky. "There are hundreds of zombies. We're outnumbered."

"We'll just do it, one at a time," Harriet said as she charged toward the zombie that stood in the doorway and pierced the vacant-eyed undead mob with her diamond sword. The others followed.

No matter how many zombies they destroyed, more seemed to spawn almost instantly.

Julian said, "There has to be a zombie spawner. We need to find it and deactivate the spawner. It's our only hope."

As the gang battled the zombies, Steve and Julian sprinted far from the wheat farm in search of the zombie spawner.

"Where could it be?" asked Julian.

Steve knew the landscape well. "it might be in this field right outside the village. It seems like zombies are coming from that direction."

"Who would do this to your town? Do you have any enemies?" asked Julian.

"There was a man who used to live here named Valentino. He has been terrorizing us ever since he left."

"Valentino!" Julian couldn't believe his ears. "We have also been battling him."

"Yes, he causes problems all over the Overworld. He seems to be everyone's enemy," Steve said breathlessly as he led Julian to the patch of land where he hoped they'd find the spawner.

Just as they reached the field, the sun came up and the zombies disappeared. Julian said, "I hope our friends are okay. I feel badly that we didn't find the spawner."

The sun shined brightly on the field. Julian spotted a book on the ground and picked it up.

"What's that?" asked Steve.

"It can't be." Julian looked at the cover. "It's another one of William's journals."

Steve was shocked. "You mean the journal I read was actually from William the Explorer?"

"Yes. It's a small portion of the journal, which is why it didn't make any sense to you. You have to read it from the beginning. We need to head back and read this to my friends. These journals are helping us find William. We're going to save him and set him free and we're going to defeat Charles."

"And Valentino," added Steve.

"Yes, we will defeat the bad guys and set William free, so he can explore the Overworld again."

Steve was excited. He wanted to help his new friends. Steve and Julian sprinted back to his wheat farm. As they raced, Julian was worried that he'd get back to the farm and find all of his friends had been destroyed. He was happy when he heard Harriet call out, "Julian!"

"Is everyone safe?" asked Julian.

"Yes." Harriet smiled.

"Look at what I found." Julian held up the book.

"Another journal! That's great!" Ezra was excited.

Julian read from the journal, and they all listened.

10
JOURNAL ENTRY: FIND ME

Entry 5: Back to the Nether

"Why don't you crawl down the hole to see if you can find them?" I asked Charles.

I knew Charles had sent most of his army to the Nether to search for resources and he wasn't as strong as he appeared. This was our opportunity to defeat Charles.

"I don't have to go down that hole. My men will find Esther and Molly. They can't escape this island." He let out another loud laugh.

I didn't want to believe him. I wanted to see him as weak. I wanted Esther and Molly to escape from the island. And I was very upset when I saw one of Charles's soldiers escort Esther and Molly back into the stronghold.

"I told you they wouldn't get far." Charles laughed even louder.

Esther and Molly walked back into the cell. They held their faces down and looked sad.

When Charles and the soldiers left, I asked Molly, "What happened?"

"The minute we climbed out of the hole, they were waiting for us," Molly replied.

Esther added, "But I saw a bunch of them on a portal to the Nether, so he doesn't have his entire army."

"I think we should try and escape again," suggested Sean.

We all looked at the hole in the ground. Charles never had us fill it in, so it was still open and ready for us to climb in. We could escape through the hole. We knew there would be soldiers at the other end who would attack us, but if we were prepared, we might have a chance to fight back.

I was the first to jump in the hole, prepared for an attack. My friends followed. I didn't want them to know how nervous I was. My heart was beating very fast. When I climbed out of the hole, I looked around, but I didn't see anyone.

"There aren't any soldiers," I told the others.

The rest of the gang climbed out. We sprinted toward the shore. We needed to find boats to take us off the island. As we raced toward the shore, a group of soldiers sprinted toward us. They shot arrows, and we tried to dodge them.

"What are we going to do?" Sean asked me.

I noticed three soldiers crafting a portal to the Nether. They were putting down the obsidian when I sprinted toward them with my diamond sword. I struck two of them. The soldiers must have been extremely weak, because I was able to defeat them with just a couple of blows from my sword.

"Help!" Esther shouted as the third solider forced her into the portal. A purple mist rose around Esther and the soldier. We could see her fighting the soldier as they disappeared and traveled to the Nether.

"We need to save her," Molly cried out,.

I looked out at the soldiers that were racing toward us. I quickly began to craft a portal to the Nether. That was our only option.

"Hop on," I called to my friends.

We stood on the portal and watched as more soldiers charged toward us. The purple mist took over, blocking the soldiers from our view. We disappeared, and they were left standing on Mushroom Island.

When we emerged in the Nether, Molly shouted, "Esther! Where are you?"

"She can be anywhere," Sean told Molly.

"Don't say that." Molly was upset. She missed her friend and she was worried that Esther was alone in the Nether with a hostile soldier.

"We'll find her. Don't worry," I comforted Molly.

We walked along a lava stream. Sean pointed out a Nether fortress in the distance. "We should see if there is treasure."

I added, "That would be a good place to search for Esther and the solider. I bet all of the soldiers are looting the Nether fortresses for Nether wart."

We sprinted toward the fortress, but stopped when a blaze's fireball landed right near us.

My heart raced. I was still fearful of fire. I grabbed a snowball from my inventory and aimed it at the yellow flying terror. I missed.

Sean shouted, "Watch out!"

I jumped back and narrowly avoided being struck by a second fireball. I didn't like this one bit. My heart beat even faster. I grabbed another snowball and threw it at the blaze. I struck the blaze and it was destroyed.

"There are more!" Molly shouted as three more blazes flew in our direction.

We armed ourselves with snowballs and threw them at the blazes while we shielded ourselves from the fiery blasts. When the final blaze was defeated, we sprinted toward the Nether fortress.

Molly raced toward the stairwell. "I knew it. There isn't any Nether wart. The soldiers have already looted the fortress."

I could hear voices. "It sounds like there is still someone lurking in this fortress."

Molly quietly peeked down the hall, and then explored the rest of the fortress. "Guys!" she called out. "Look who I found!"

Esther was relieved to see us.

"Are you okay?" I asked her.

"Yes. I defeated the solider. But there are more. We have to get out of here," she told us.

"But where should we go?" asked Sean.

"We need to back to the Overworld and defeat Charles, or this will never end," I told them.

They agreed. But we still didn't have a plan. We left the fortress, and as we walked outside, I was surprised when I heard a familiar voice.

11
NOT THE NETHER

We have a change of plans. We aren't going to Mushroom Island. We're going to the Nether," Harriet announced.

Julian put down the journal and said, "Well, we aren't going anywhere until we help Steve and his village fight this zombie invasion. Did you guys know that Valentino is behind these attacks?"

Veronica cried out, "Valentino? Are you sure??"

"Yes, Valentino is the one who has been attacking us," confirmed Steve.

"We must stop him," said Julian.

The sky grew dark and rain fell on the town. Steve said, "This means the zombies will be here soon. We have to go help the village."

The gang ran through the rainy town. They saw zombies lumbering toward the village.

Julian said, "We need to back to the area where we found the journal. We have to search for the spawner."

The group sprinted toward the field outside of the village. It wasn't an easy journey, and they almost didn't make it. A cluster of zombies surrounded them and they had to battle their way out. Julian's energy level was dangerously low and he used his last bit of energy to strike a vacant-eyed zombie. He needed help. If a zombie struck him he'd be destroyed.

Harriet noticed Julian's cry for help. She lunged at the zombie that attacked Julian. She struck the undead beast with her diamond sword and obliterated the hostile mob.

"Thanks," Julian said weakly.

Harriet handed Julian a bottle of milk. "Drink this. It will help you get your strength back."

The final zombie was defeated and the gang continued to the area where Julian and Steve had found the journal.

Steve shouted, "I see the spawner."

The gang sprinted toward Steve and they worked together to quickly destroy the spawner.

"It's deactivated!" Steve cried with tears of joy.

The gang sprinted back into town. The sun came out, and the gang walked over to the half-built golem. Harriet looked at the iron golem. "We don't have that much left to do. Let's finish it now and then head to the Nether."

They all agreed and began to work on the golem. In a matter of minutes, the iron golem was constructed and the townspeople came out to celebrate. A villager walked over to the gang and said, "Thank you so much for helping our town. We are grateful for all that you have done for us."

"We're glad we could help." Harriet smiled.

"But now it's time for us to go," said Julian. "It's been nice meeting you all and we really like your town."

Jack said, "We know that your town is being attacked by Valentino. We want you to know that we are working to defeat Valentino. We want to stop him from terrorizing the Overworld."

Veronica added, "I know Valentino and I know how awful he can be to people. I also vow to stop him and save the Overworld."

The villagers and townspeople applauded.

Harriet began to craft a portal to the Nether. Before she stepped on the portal and ignited it, she looked over at Steve. "Would you like to join us on our journey?"

Steve paused. He didn't know how to respond. He finally replied, "I'd love to, but I think it's better for me to stay here and protect my town. I don't trust Valentino and I know he will be back. I wouldn't feel comfortable helping you when I was worried about my town."

Oliver looked at Steve and said, "You're doing the right thing."

Steve was honored that Oliver respected his decision. "Oliver, I can't believe I even got to meet you. Meeting you was one of the greatest moments of my life."

Oliver blushed. "That means a lot to me."

Steve asked, "When you are reunited with William, will you both come to this town to visit us?"

"Yes," Oliver promised.

Then Harriet called out, "I ignited the portal."

Oliver sprinted toward the portal and hopped on. Within seconds they were in the fiery red Nether. Two ghasts flew toward them. Oliver used his fist and punched a fireball and it destroyed the ghast. Harriet destroyed the second ghast, and then breathlessly said, "Welcome back to the Nether. It seems like the fun never ends here."

"Don't joke." Veronica was annoyed. She didn't want to return to the Nether.

"We're on a mission," Oliver reminded them. "William might be trapped down here and we must find him."

"Where should we look?" asked Toby.

Harriet spotted a Nether fortress in the distance. "I think we should start with that fortress."

The group sprinted toward the Nether fortress. There were three blazes defending it. The gang grabbed snowballs from their inventories and threw them at the blazes. It didn't take long, but soon all of the blazes were destroyed. The gang raced inside the fortress.

Harriet noticed the Nether wart growing out of the patch of soul sand on the side of the staircase. "This is the same Nether fortress where William found Esther. It hasn't been looted."

Jack said, "I bet there is treasure here."

Ezra was annoyed. "This is no time to search for treasure. We need to focus and find William. I'm sure there are countless fortresses in the Nether. We have to find the one that William was in."

"That's impossible," said Veronica. "We've been looking for William for a long time. It isn't that easy."

Harriet saw a book on the floor. "Maybe we aren't so far off course."

"Another journal?" asked Julian.

"It looks like it," Harriet said as she leafed through the book.

"I wonder how it wound up in this Nether fortress," pondered Julian.

"I don't know, but we have to read it. It's the only way we can find William," Harriet told the group.

"But we've read about a million entries from his journal and we still haven't found him," said Toby.

"Maybe this will be the one that leads us to him." Harriet was hopeful and she began to read.

12
JOURNAL ENTRY: LANDSLIDE

Entry 6: Out of the Fire

Charles stood outside the Nether fortress. I was ready to confront him. I didn't use words. I simply leapt at Charles and struck him with my diamond sword. After the initial blow, I shouted, "Stop it. This has gone on far too long."

"You escaped and you thought you were going to get away with it?" Charles was angry.

"You couldn't keep us prisoner forever. I want to find my friend Oliver. I want to explore the Overworld." Again, I struck Charles with my diamond sword and saw that he was losing hearts. He was growing weak.

Charles only had a handful of soldiers with him. This wasn't going to be a tough battle. My friends battled the soldiers as I fought Charles. The battle was interrupted when three blazes flew toward us. We all tried to avoid getting hit by the fireballs, but one of Charles's soldiers was struck. Then another was destroyed.

"No!" Charles shouted as he watched two of his soldiers disappear.

"You're losing your army," I shouted as I struck Charles with his diamond sword.

Molly grabbed snowballs from her inventory and threw them at the blazes. She destroyed one blaze.

"Good job!" Thao called out.

"Watch out!" Esther shouted to Thao.

Thao looked up, but he didn't see the fireball headed in his direction. The fireball destroyed him.

"Thao!" I shouted. I was upset that my friend had been destroyed. I knew he'd respawn on Mushroom Island. At least we hadn't slept in the prison. He would respawn in the lavish house he had built with Molly and Esther. But he was still gone, and I wanted to be reunited with him. We had to get out of the Nether.

I didn't have that much strength left, and I had to battle Charles without getting destroyed from a blaze's fireball. Molly and Esther were working hard to destroy the blazes and dodge the fireballs, but the hostile mobs were still flying through the Nether sky.

"We need help!" Molly called out.

Sean was battling two soldiers. I was fighting Charles. Molly threw another snowball and destroyed the blaze.

"There's one blaze left!" Esther was happy.

"We can defeat it," Molly said and then added, "But I only have one snowball left in my inventory."

Sean destroyed another soldier. Charles was devastated and shouted, "No, not another soldier!"

Esther destroyed the final blaze. Sean destroyed the last soldier. We were alone with Charles. We surrounded him.

"You better surrender now!" I shouted at Charles.

We thought he would give up. We thought we had finally won. But we were surprised when Charles laughed. He grabbed a potion of invisibility from his inventory and splashed it on himself. Just like that, he was gone.

"What happened?" Sean asked.

"He is extremely tricky." I was annoyed. I wanted this battle to end, but I also wanted to find Thao. I knew he was on Mushroom Island. "We need to make a portal back to the Overworld. We must find Thao."

Everyone agreed, although we knew traveling to Mushroom Island would be quite dangerous. We didn't want to get trapped in the stronghold. Since the island was desolate and removed from the rest of the Overworld, we'd have no help. We could get trapped there forever.

"I'm going to craft the portal," Molly announced.

"Great," I said, "We'll help you."

We helped Molly craft the portal and we hopped into it. As purple mist surrounded us, I smiled. I was happy to be out of the Nether.

"Watch out!" Molly shouted as we emerged in the Overworld in the middle of the night. Two Endermen carrying blocks walked past us. Molly warned, "Don't look at them. We don't want them to attack us."

I tried to avoid eye contact with the lanky mobs, but it was too late. One of them had seen me and let out a piercing shriek. As it teleported toward me, my heart raced. I was going to be destroyed.

"Sprint toward the water," Esther called out.

I looked around. I didn't see any water. It was so dark that I couldn't see anything.

Molly shouted, "The water is over here. Sprint! Follow me!"

I sprinted toward Molly and followed her to the water. I jumped in the deep blue ocean as the Enderman chased me. The second Enderman followed, and both of them jumped in the water, where they were quickly destroyed. I swam back to the shore.

"This is going to be hard. We respawned at night. There are way too many hostile mobs that can spawn." Sean was worried. He looked around for more Endermen and other creatures of the night.

"I wish I had Oliver here, he was a map expert. He could lead us anywhere at anytime." I said.

"Even in the middle of the night?" asked Molly.

"Yes," I replied.

As we walked slowly through the grassy biome, we kept watch for hostile mobs. I was shocked when I heard a voice cry out in the distance.

"Help!" the voice called.

"That sounds like Charles," I told the others.

A second voice shouted, "You're not going to win!"

"That sounds like Thao!" Molly called out.

We sprinted in the dark, trying to not to trip, as we made our way toward the two familiar voices.

13
SURPRISE IN THE MINE

We don't know where they are." Harriet was upset.

"They could be anywhere in the Overworld," Ezra said.

"We need to get out of the Nether," Oliver remarked.

"And fast!" Toby cried as three ghasts flew toward them.

One ghast shot a fireball at Harriet. She used her fist to deflect the fireball and destroy the fiery mob. The others battled the remaining ghasts.

"The Nether is a death trap. We have to get out of here," Oliver announced as he started to craft a portal back to the Overworld.

The gang hopped into the portal and purple mist rose around them. Within seconds they emerged in the middle of the swamp. A bat flew by Toby's head. He ducked to avoid it. "I don't like it here," Toby called out.

"Me too," Veronica complained. "I hate the swamp."

71

Harriet told everyone to be quiet. "I hear something."

Boing! Boing! Boing!

"I hear it, too! What's that noise?" cried Julian.

Boing! Boing! Boing!

"It sounds like slimes!" Veronica called out.

Harriet saw four slimes bounce toward them. "Yes! I see slimes. Everyone get out your swords."

The gang battled the slimes, but it was tough. The bouncy, slimy creatures broke into smaller slimes, making destroying them particularly tricky. The gang worked hard to obliterate the smaller slimes with their diamond swords. It was an intense battle, and just when they thought it was over, a witch appeared. The purple-robed witch clutched a vile of potion in one hand and sprinted toward the group. She splashed a potion on Harriet.

Ezra raced toward the witch and struck her with his diamond sword. "Help!" he called out to the others.

Julian shot an arrow at the witch.

Veronica ran to Harriet and gave her some milk. "Take this. It will make you feel better."

Harriet drank the milk as she watched her friends destroy the witch. "We have to get out of the swamp."

"I think we all agree with you," Julian said as the gang hurried through the swampy biome toward a mountain.

"It's almost night," Veronica pointed out. "We need to build a house."

The gang agreed and they found a patch of land by the mountain and constructed a home.

"We are becoming experts at crafting quick homes," Harriet remarked as they placed a door on the house.

Julian sighed, "These are skills I never wanted to have. I just wish I was back on my wheat farm. I want to stop searching for William. I want us to find him soon."

"We all feel the same way," Harriet replied. "Maybe tomorrow is the day we find him."

They hadn't given up hope that they would find him, but they were all exhausted. They climbed into bed and spent another night dreaming of finding William.

The sun began to rise and they prepared themselves for the trek up the mountain.

As they walked toward the mountain, Harriet pointed out, "I see a cave."

"Do you think we should go mining?" Veronica asked. She was confused.

"Yes, we can find diamonds and other valuable minerals," Harriet said. "We don't know where William is. I feel like our journey might be over. If we don't find another journal, William might be lost in the Overworld. He will have to escape from Charles on his own."

Oliver didn't like hearing that at all and said, "We can't just give up on William. We will find another journal and we will free William."

Toby agreed and reminded them, "You know we found the first journal in an abandoned mineshaft. Maybe we'll find another journal in this cave."

Harriet added, "We can mine and look."

The group was divided. Half of them wanted to go in the cave and the other half felt that it was a waste of time.

"Mining in a cave is too dangerous and takes too long." Jack was annoyed.

Harriet was persistent. "We need to go mining. I want us to have a fully stocked inventory. It's the only way we can survive this journey if we're going to keep searching."

Veronica added, "It would be a shame to pass up an opportunity to go mining. It's been a while since we spotted a cave, and I want to see what we can find."

Harriet and Veronica entered the cave. They didn't look back to see who was following them.

Jack called out, "Harriet and Veronica! Seriously? You are just going to mine without voting on whether or not we should enter the cave?"

Harriet stopped. "Okay, let's vote."

The group voted. The majority of the gang chose to explore the cave. Jack let out a loud sigh. They could tell he was annoyed. Harriet said, "We voted. It was fair. Now we get to explore the cave."

The cave was dark. Julian spotted a cave spider and struck it with his sword. The group dug into the ground with their pickaxes. Ezra called out, "More spiders!"

"There must be a spawner somewhere." Harriet looked for the spawner, but didn't see it.

"I think I see it!" exclaimed Julian.

The gang sprinted to Julian's side. Oliver said, "I see it. We have to destroy it."

They used torches to disable the spawner. When it was deactivated, they resumed mining in the cave. They dug their pickaxes deep into the bottom of the cave, but there weren't any minerals.

"Where are the diamonds?" Harriet called out. She was annoyed, and she had been the one who had suggested they go mining.

"Just keep digging and we'll find them," Veronica said as she reached another layer underneath the ground and found nothing.

Julian climbed out of the hole. He was tired and needed a break. He grabbed an apple from his inventory and took a bite.

Oliver called out, "Julian, are you eating? We need help."

Julian looked down and saw a book in the corner of the cave. "Guys!" he called out. "I see a book."

The gang jumped from the hole and sprinted toward the book. Oliver reached over and picked it up. "It's another journal!"

"Now are you guys upset that I wanted us to mine in this cave?" Harriet said as she peeked over Oliver's shoulder and looked at the journal.

"There's no time to talk about that," Jack said. "Oliver, read."

Oliver started to read from the journal.

14

JOURNAL ENTRY: REUNITED

Entry 7: Victories

We sprinted in the dark toward the voices. I called out, "Thao!" But there wasn't a reply.

"Do you think we were imagining it?" asked Molly.

"No," I replied breathlessly.

Sean stopped and shouted, "Oh no!"

My heart sank. In front of us stood the largest army of skeletons I've ever seen. They surrounded Charles and Thao and were shooting arrows at them.

"What are going to do?" Esther asked. "There are so many skeletons. We can never battle them all."

I grabbed my sword. "We have to try. We need to save Thao."

We sprinted toward our friend while we shielded ourselves from skeleton attacks.

"Help!" Thao called out. His energy was incredibly low and he was desperate.

Sean splashed potions on the skeletons, which weakened them. I used this opportunity to destroy as many weak skeletons as I could, but the battle seemed pointless. There were too many skeletons.

I was shocked when Molly reached Charles and he struck her with his diamond sword. I thought he'd use his last bits of strength to fight the skeletons. Molly was about to strike Charles when I shouted, "Don't attack him. We want him to live so we can find Oliver."

Charles shouted, "You'll never find Oliver. I am not revealing where he is being held prisoner. I'd rather be destroyed by you guys than help Oliver escape."

Sean cried for help. "These skeletons are going to destroy me!"

I was conflicted. I wanted to destroy the skeletons, but I also wanted to confront Charles. This had to end. I sprinted toward Charles and aimed my sword at him. I demanded, "You had better tell us where Oliver is being kept prisoner."

Charles laughed.

"Why are you laughing?" I asked Charles.

"Look behind you." Charles let out another laugh.

I turned around and saw his army fighting the skeletons. The sun began to rise and the skeletons disappeared. We had to fight Charles's army. I sprinted toward a soldier with my diamond sword, but he wasn't easy to fight. Charles had a strong army of skilled fighters.

I looked over at Molly and Esther as they destroyed a bunch of soldiers. This infuriated Charles. He sprinted toward them with his sword.

Molly shielded herself from his sword and struck Charles. Again, I warned her not to destroy Charles. She called out, "There's no other way."

The fight continued, but we were losing. Charles called out, "Let us stop battling now. If you are destroyed, I have soldiers stationed at the last place you slept. There is no escaping me. You must surrender now."

I didn't know what to do. There was a possibility that Charles wasn't telling the truth. I looked over at my friends. They also looked confused.

I decided to battle Charles. I wasn't going to be kept prisoner again. I'd rather respawn and try to fight his army than give myself up. Molly was destroying a lot of soldiers and we had a chance of winning. I will admit, it was a small chance, but it was still a chance.

I struck Charles with my sword.

Charles called out, "Valentino!"

I saw a man sprint toward Charles with more soldiers. Valentino raced over to me and hit me with his diamond sword.

"You're coming with me," Valentino demanded.

I was too weak to fight. I followed Valentino. Charles made the others follow us. We walked toward the desert. I hoped they would put us in a prison with Oliver. We approached a large desert temple. It looked familiar and I realized this was the temple where Oliver, Julian, and I had found the treasure.

"This way," Charles said as he led down the stairs into a stronghold that was underneath the desert temple.

As I walked down the long dark hall deep beneath the temple, I was hoping I'd hear Oliver's voice, but it was silent.

Charles stopped in front of a door and laughed. "This is where you'll be staying. Forever. Don't try and escape. This time I am clearing your inventories."

I struck Charles with my sword. I wasn't going to give up everything in my inventory. "Never!" I shouted at Charles.

One of Charles soldiers asked him, "Should I use the command blocks to put them on Hardcore mode?"

Charles paused. "Not yet."

I froze. I couldn't believe Charles wanted to destroy us. I had to escape. I lunged at him again.

"Stop!" Charles called out. "I won't put you on Hardcore mode if you just follow the rules."

I looked over at my friends. We walked into the prison cell.

"I think they're gone," Sean said, "I don't hear anything."

"How could be we trapped again? This is awful," Esther was very upset.

"We will get out of here," I told them. "I'm sure of it."

Sean paced the small room. "We don't even have anything in our inventories. Planning an escape seems pointless."

I stared at the ground. "Look at that."

Molly walked over to me. "Wow, a book."

Esther said, "Is it an enchantment book? I mean it's not like we have anything to enchant."

Thao said, "All of our inventories are empty."

Sean looked at it more carefully. "It's a journal."

I wondered if it was an old journal of mine that Charles had gotten his hands on. I asked Sean, "Read the journal."

Sean said, "It says it's Oliver's journal."

I was shocked and blurted out, "This is where they must have kept him."

Molly said, "Maybe he escaped."

My thoughts were a lot grimmer. I worried that Charles had put Oliver on Hardcore mode. I was upset and wanted Sean to read the journal so we could get more information.

Sean began to read.

15
GETTING CLOSER

We know where they are!" Harriet called out.

"We need to go back to the desert!" Ezra was excited.

"Do you have a map?" Julian asked Oliver.

Oliver was thrilled. "Yes, I have a map!"

The gang sprinted out of the cave and followed Oliver up the mountain. The energy level was high. Everyone was excited. They finally knew where William was being held prisoner.

"What did you write in your journal?" Harriet asked Oliver.

"I wrote about being trapped in the room. It was a horrible existence and I didn't think I'd ever escape until you guys found me. I think William feels he has more of a chance of escaping because he has friends with him. I was alone and starving and had nothing."

"That sounds awful," said Harriet.

Oliver stopped at the peak of the mountain and pointed to the desert. "That is where I was trapped. We are almost there. We will set William free soon."

The gang carefully made their way down the side of the mountain, and walked into a thick jungle. Oliver cleared a path for the group.

Harriet was worried they'd lose each other. "The path is thick with leaves. I hope we can all stick together."

"I'll make sure we won't lose each other," Oliver said quite confidently.

"Watch out!" Julian warned everyone.

Charles's army sprinted toward them. The soldiers shot arrows at the group. The gang tried to dodge the arrows, but one pierced Jack's arm.

"Ouch!" Jack cried.

"We have to fight these soldiers," ordered Harriet. "We are too close to saving William. We must use all of our tricks to win this battle."

The group shot arrows and used their swords to battle the army, but they were outnumbered and the battle was making them weak.

Harriet smiled when she saw a creeper silently walk toward a group of soldiers and explode.

Kaboom!

More creepers appeared and destroyed the soldiers.

Ezra said, "I bet Charles summoned the creepers to attack us and it backfired."

They used the creeper invasion to escape from the soldiers, sprinting through the jungle, trying to hide behind the leaves as we trekked through the lush jungle.

"I see a jungle temple," Veronica called out.

"We can't go in there. We have to make our way to the desert fast," said Harriet.

Ezra looked back. "There are still soldiers following us. Maybe we should hide in the temple. We can't run straight to the desert. They will follow us the entire way."

The group reluctantly sprinted toward the temple, making sure the soldiers didn't see them enter the grand temple. Harriet looked out from the temple's entrance and saw the soldiers sprint by them.

Harriet was relieved. "I think coming here was a good idea. It looks as if they think we are still running to the desert."

Oliver was worried. "I hope they don't panic and put William on Hardcore mode."

Julian remarked, "That would be awful."

"We are going to save William," declared Harriet. "We are also going to defeat both Charles and Valentino and this entire battle will be over."

The group was hopeful, but they were worried about William. They were so close to saving him.

Veronica stood by the entrance to the jungle temple, "I don't see any soldiers. They're all gone. We should leave and go to the desert."

Nobody suggested that they search for treasure. Everyone was agreed that they should go back to the desert.

The gang looked in every direction as they searched for soldiers. When they confirmed that the jungle was empty, they sprinted toward the desert.

Harriet warned, "We should also keep watch for creepers. I'm sure Charles is spawning them."

The jungle was immense and the group felt as if they were sprinting forever. As the followed Oliver, who sheared a path through the dense leaves, they were all excited and hopeful they would find William soon.

"We will finally meet Sean, Molly, Esther, and Thao," Harriet said to the gang.

Oliver reminded them, "I've met Thao. He wasn't always nice."

"I just want to defeat Charles and Valentino," Veronica said. "They have caused the Overworld too much trouble."

They could see the desert. "We're almost there! I can't believe it!" Toby exclaimed.

The minute they stepped onto the sandy biome, a sea of arrows flooded them and they heard a loud sinister laugh. "You think you're going to save your friend?" Charles called out to them.

"I don't think we are going to save him. I know we are going to save him," Harriet replied.

"How do you know I didn't destroy him? I could have used command blocks to put him on Hardcore mode and destroy him." Charles laughed.

"You aren't that bad," Oliver said.

"You don't think I'm bad, Oliver?" Charles was perplexed. "I kept you as a prisoner for years."

"And you never destroyed me on Hardcore mode. So why would you do that to William?"

Charles wasn't sure he was following Oliver's logic. He said, "And you escaped. I didn't want William escaping like you did."

"I didn't just escape. These friends saved me, and I will do the same for William. You have kept too many prisoners. You have no right to do that." With those last words, Oliver held his diamond sword against Charles's chest.

Harriet shot an arrow at Charles. Ezra sprinted toward the soldiers with his diamond sword. It was a full-blown battle. Harriet could see the desert temple in the distance. She hoped William and his friends were still in there. As she lunged at a soldier, she wondered how much longer they'd have to battle. She wanted to free William.

Valentino sprinted toward the group with his sword. He leapt at Veronica. Harriet joined Veronica and helped her defeat Valentino before he could cause any trouble.

"Your sidekick is gone," Harriet called out to Charles.

He turned around and cried, "Valentino!"

16
JOURNAL ENTRY: WE WILL ESCAPE

Entry 8: Setbacks

We read Oliver's journal, but it said nothing about escaping. It just talked about living in solitude in the prison. It was a hard read. I spent the entire time choking back tears. I assumed Charles put Oliver on Hardcore mode one day and the idea that he spent his final years just sitting in a prison was heartbreaking. Oliver chronicled what it was like to be weak and hungry. I couldn't bear to read the journal. I felt for my friend. I wished I could have helped him. I tried, but it was too late. Molly could see that I was very upset.

"I'm sorry," Molly said. "I know he was your best friend."

Sean vowed, "We will escape and we will defeat Charles. He won't get away with this."

I wasn't sure Sean was right. I knew that Charles had a lot of power and he could put us on Hardcore mode and he'd win. But I had to be hopeful. I had to imagine that Oliver escaped, even though I knew that was almost impossible.

Esther looked at me, "I think once we escape, we'll feel better. Let's come up with a plan."

"How?" I asked. I knew this question would upset them. They often looked to me for direction. I was the great world explorer and now I had nothing to offer them. I was ready to give up, and they noticed.

"We can dig a hole and escape," suggested Sean.

I replied, "With what supplies? Charles emptied our inventories."

"I was able to hide something in my inventory." Sean took out a pickaxe. We were all shocked.

Esther asked, "Do you have energy to dig?"

"Yes," Sean said, and he began to dig a hole in the center of the room.

"I can't believe you had a pickaxe. This is fantastic." I stood by Sean. I wanted to help him, but he only had one pickaxe.

"This will take forever." Molly looked down at the small hole. "We just can't let Sean do all of the work."

Sean was losing energy. "You're right. And I don't have enough strength to finish it."

Molly took the pickaxe and dug it into the ground. "Maybe we can take turns."

"I think this might be pointless," I told them. "Even if we take turns, we will just lose more energy and we have no way to replenish the supply. Charles hasn't left any food for us and we have no idea if he put us on Hardcore mode. I don't want any of us to get destroyed."

"What are we going to do? I refuse to be trapped in this prison." Sean was angry and he paced in the small jail cell.

"Stop pacing," I warned him. "You'll run out of energy. Just stand still."

Sean couldn't stop pacing. He was thinking and plotting our way out of the prison.

Molly looked up at the ceiling. "Do you think it would be easier to escape through the ceiling?"

"No," I said. "There's no way we'll reach the ceiling and it probably would just leave us in the desert temple and we'd be marched back down here."

We had no plans. We were losing hope. We couldn't even hear Charles or the soldiers. I wondered if they had abandoned us. They were waiting for us to run out of energy and be destroyed.

Sean continued to pace. "When is Charles going to give us food?"

"Hopefully soon," I said. "It's been awhile."

Molly announced, "My food bar is very low. If I don't eat soon, I might be destroyed."

"But what if he put us on Hardcore mode?" Esther panicked. She was worried this was the end.

"What should we do?" Sean was anxious.

"We need to calm down. I will think of a plan," I told them. But I didn't have a plan.

And I didn't have time to think, because Thao shouted, "A spider!"

Sean used his pickaxe to destroy the red-eyed beast.

"We can't have any other mobs spawn in here or we are ruined." I didn't know what to do.

I looked through Oliver's journal, rereading the entries and hoping I would find some clues. Maybe the journal would give us some tips on how to escape—maybe I had missed a clue.

Thao shouted again. "Another spider!"

Sean destroyed it with his pickaxe. "Thankfully I have this pickaxe, but I can't keep fighting these insects. I'm getting weak."

I called to the others. "It looks like there might be a way to escape from this prison. Oliver talked about a planned escape through a tunnel."

"A tunnel?" Sean sprinted toward my side.

"How are we going to dig a tunnel?" asked Thao.

I heard voices. "Shhh! I hear someone."

We were silent. I listened to the muffled voices. One particular voice sounded very familiar.

17
SAVING FRIENDS

Charles's army was weakening, and without Valentino, he was losing the battle.

Harriet struck Charles with her diamond sword and he was destroyed. "Let's go to the desert temple!" she called out to her friends.

The gang sprinted toward the desert temple. When they entered the temple, three soldiers leapt toward them. One of the soldiers struck Harriet with his diamond sword.

Ezra jumped in front of Harriet and battled the soldier. "Go find William," Ezra told Harriet. "I can fight."

"You're not going to fight alone," Harriet told him.

The gang battled the three soldiers and destroyed them, but more emerged. Julian looked out at the group of soldiers dressed in black. "I don't think this is going to be an easy battle." Julian shot arrows at the soldiers.

Kaboom!

There was an explosion. Harriet called out, "Creepers!"

Two creepers silently crept behind the soldiers and exploded. Ezra said, "We have to watch out for the creepers. I bet Charles is still summoning them."

Veronica stuck a soldier with her diamond sword when Valentino sprinted into the room.

Valentino warned, "You're not going to win this battle and you won't save your friends."

"Yes, we will!" Veronica raced toward Valentino and struck him with her sword until he was destroyed.

Oliver called out, "The stronghold where I was prisoner is right over here."

"We won't let you get into the stronghold," one of the soldiers shouted at the gang.

Harriet struck the solider with her sword. The army was growing weak. The gang drank milk to replenish their energy, helping them to defeat the army. When the final soldier was destroyed, Oliver sprinted toward the hole in the ground and climbed in. Everyone followed him down into the stronghold. When they reached the stronghold, they saw Charles.

"What do you think you're doing?" Charles let out a loud laugh.

"Saving our friends." Harriet stood in front of Charles.

"You don't even know William. He isn't your friend." Charles held his diamond sword against Harriet's chest.

"I know that the Overworld will be thrilled to have William the Explorer chronicling his expeditions. You have kept him prisoner for too long!" Harriet shouted.

Oliver stood by Harriet and lunged at Charles with his sword. "You aren't going to stop us this time. You're our prisoner now."

Charles laughed. "The soldiers will respawn soon and you'll never get away with it."

Valentino sprinted down the hall. "They won't respawn. I accidently put them on Hardcore mode. They are gone."

"You fool!" Charles shouted at Valentino.

"I'm sorry," Valentino cried.

"You've destroyed my army," Charles shouted.

A creeper silently crept behind Charles and exploded. *Kaboom!*

"Oh no!" Valentino called out. "He was on Hardcore mode, too!"

"What about William and the others?" Harriet asked.

"No! I mean—I don't know!" Valentino was confused.

Harriet demanded, "Lead us to the command blocks."

The gang followed Valentino down a dimly lit hall. A spider emerged from a corner and Harriet destroyed it with one blow from her diamond sword.

"Here are the command blocks," Valentino showed them. "What should I do?"

Harriet destroyed them and then announced, "We have some friends to save."

Veronica asked, "But what do we do with Valentino?"

Harriet replied, "Valentino, you must be punished for what you have done to the Overworld. We have visited towns that you have destroyed with nightly zombie attacks. Everything you have done has hurt others."

"I'm sorry," Valentino said with his head down.

"Once we free our friends, we will bring you to the town that you have damaged and you will be placed in a prison in the town," Harriet informed him.

Valentino stood quietly. There was nothing else he could do. He had no backup and he had no way to escape. Ezra and Julian walked next to Valentino and pointed their swords at him.

Ezra warned, "Don't even try to find a way to escape."

The gang sprinted down the hall toward William. They reached his prison cell and Harriet hit the wall with her pickaxe.

"We need to free them," Harriet shouted.

"We're here!" Oliver called out to his friends as he banged his pickaxe against the prison wall.

18
JOURNAL ENTRY:
IT'S THE END

Entry 9: The Best Day

"Oliver!" I called out.

"Yes, William!" he shouted out from the other side of the wall.

"Save us!" I cried.

"We will," he replied.

A woman broke down the wall with her pickaxe and set us free. She said, "My name is Harriet." She then introduced us to her large group of friends. I spotted Julian.

"Julian!" I called out.

"It has been too long, my old friend."

A woman named Veronica smiled. "The Overworld will be pleased to have you back in action, William. I can't wait to read about your adventures."

"Thanks," I replied. I was overwhelmed.

"How did you find us?" Sean asked.

Harriet explained, "I was in an abandoned mineshaft with my friends Jack and Toby and we found your first journal. The cover said we'd be cursed if we read it, but we wanted to find you."

"I'm so glad you did," I replied. I remembered when I wrote that first entry. I didn't want anyone reading my personal thoughts, so I warned any reader they'd be cursed.

"We are so happy that we found you," Harriet smiled.

I looked over at Valentino. "What are you doing here?"

Harriet announced, "He is coming back with us. We are placing him in a prison."

I was happy to hear Valentino would be punished. I looked over at everyone. "Thank you for searching for us."

We exited the prison and walked through the desert temple and into the desert. The sun was shining brightly.

Oliver looked at his map. "This is the way to the town."

I didn't even ask him where we were going. I just wanted to enjoy the sun and the freedom. It was all over. We were finally able to explore the Overworld again. We followed Oliver over a mountain. When we reached the top of the mountain, I asked everyone to stop. I looked at the Overworld. "The view is so beautiful. I can't wait to start exploring again."

We headed down the mountain and toward a small village. Harriet led us to a wheat farm and knocked on the door of the farmhouse. A man opened the door.

"Harriet!" he called out.

"Steve, look at who we have with us," Harriet said and pointed to me.

I introduced myself. "I'm William."

"I know who you are. I'm so glad you're free," said Steve.

Harriet then said, "We also have Valentino. And we need to put him in a prison."

Steve walked us to the center of town. He stood in the middle of the village and called out, "We have captured Valentino."

Townspeople emerged from their houses and were jubilant. They applauded. One townsperson announced there would be a feast.

Steve said, "And my friends have also found William and Oliver, the great explorers. This is a historic day in our town."

Townspeople came up to me and told me how much they loved hearing about my explorations and how glad they were that I was back. I was overjoyed. I looked over at Oliver and smiled. I was ready to explore.

DO YOU LIKE FICTION FOR MINECRAFTERS?

Check out other unofficial Minecrafter adventures from Sky Pony Press!

Invasion of the
Overworld
MARK CHEVERTON

Battle for the
Nether
MARK CHEVERTON

Confronting the
Dragon
MARK CHEVERTON

Trouble in
Zombie-town
MARK CHEVERTON

The Quest for
the Diamond
Sword
WINTER MORGAN

The Mystery
of the Griefer's
Mark
WINTER MORGAN

The Endermen
Invasion
WINTER MORGAN

Treasure
Hunters in
Trouble
WINTER MORGAN

Available wherever books are sold!

LIKE OUR BOOKS
FOR MINECRAFTERS?

Then check out other novels
by Sky Pony Press.

Pack of Dorks
BETH VRABEL

**Boys Camp:
Zack's Story**
CAMERON DOKEY,
CRAIG ORBACK

**Boys Camp:
Nate's Story**
KITSON JAZYNKA,
CRAIG ORBACK

**Letters from an
Alien Schoolboy**
R. L. ASQUITH

**Just a Drop of
Water**
KERRY O'MALLEY
CERRA

Future Flash
KITA HELMETAG
MURDOCK

Sky Run
ALEX SHEARER

Mr. Big
CAROL AND MATT
DEMBICKI

Available wherever books are sold!